Running the Road to ABC

Running the Road to ABC

BY
Denizé Lauture

ILLUSTRATED BY
Reynold Ruffins

ALADDIN PAPERBACKS

First Aladdin Paperbacks edition January 2000

Text copyright © 1996 by Denize Lauture
Illustrations copyright © 1996 by Reynold Ruffins

Aladdin Paperbacks
An imprint of Simon & Schuster Children's Publishing Division
1230 Avenue of the Americas
New York, NY 10020

Also available in a Simon & Schuster Books for Young Readers hardcover edition.
Book design by Lucille Chomowicz.
The text of this book is set in Hiroshige book.
The illustrations are rendered in gouache.
Manufactured in China
10

The Library of Congress has cataloged the hardcover edition as follows:
Lauture, Denizé
Running the road to ABC / by Denizé Lauture ;
illustrated by Reynold Ruffins
p. cm.
Summary: Long before the sun even thinks of rising the Haitian children run to school
where they learn the letters, sounds, and words of their beautiful books.
ISBN 978-0-689-80507-3
1. Blacks—Haiti—Juvenile fiction. [1. Blacks—Haiti—Fiction.
2. Haiti—Fiction. 3. Schools—Fiction.]
I. Ruffins, Reynold, ill. II. Title.
PZ7.L9185Ru 1996 [E]—dc20 95-38290 CIP AC

ISBN 978-0-689-83165-2 (pbk.)
0612 SCP

To all children who, smiling and laughing,

laughing and singing, singing and smiling,

stand tall at the golden thresholds of their lives

and welcome learning and teaching,

and teaching and learning,

as the two most endearing experiences in life.

To Robert Snadowsky, Darlene Marshall,

and editor Pamela D. Pollack,

whose gentle kindness and thoughtfulness

brought about the creation of this book.

And to my children, Conrad and Charles.

—D. L.

To Rebecca and Ranger, Seth and Alex

—R. R.

The boys are Dyesèl, Milsen, Preneyis. The girls are Loud, Kousou, Toutoun. Boys and girls are schoolchildren. They go up and down steep hills six days each week, forty weeks each year, for seven years of their short lives.

When beautiful hens still dream about handsome roosters, when handsome roosters still dream about beautiful hens, their moms wake up the boys and girls. With matchsticks and pine tree twigs the women light their kitchen fires. They cook cornmeal or millet, yam or sweet potato with Congo beans. They cook plantain or yucca with herring. The children eat their breakfasts and leave for school at dawn.

They go barefoot. Their feet remember the way in the dark. They wear blue denim shirts and short pants. Their hands hold book bags that they make themselves with palm tree leaves. Their hands hold little metal bowls of food for midday lunch, each one tied up with an embroidered cloth. Their hands swing back and forth as they run.

Their legs take cold showers of morning dew on the weeds
along the narrow trails. The bottoms of their feet flatten spiders
and slugs, and frogs and bugs they catch sleeping on the hard road.

Local folks, on the road early, step aside to make way for their rushing feet.

They begin to run long before the sun even thinks of rising. All around them they hear the *peyee-peyee* of the crickets, and the *twee-twee* of the half-awake lizards, and the *kwott-kwott* of the frogs in hollow tree trunks.

They run by the slopes of coffee trees and the meadows of corn plants, the gardens of millet and the acres of sugarcane. They run over the sweet-potato mounds like fish dancing with sea waves. They dash across dangerous crossroads, leap over mapou tree roots where hunting snakes sleep and dream. They climb slippery hills and go down rocky cliffs.

When they reach the main road, they all turn their sweaty necks and glance back. If the sun is still asleep, all of them smile, and keep the pace. But if they notice that the sky, and the hillcrests, and the treetops begin to take the color of honey, they quicken the pace. Sunlight and shade are their only clocks.

They run and run. They leave behind the ladies
urging on the donkeys bent under too-heavy loads.

They run and run. They leave behind the rich merchants whose mules rebel and kick halfway up the steep hills. They run and run.

They leave behind the bread sellers rushing to keep
their breads hot for their customers. They run and run.
Only the horse tamers keep up with them.

They even outrace the townsfolk's jeeps and trucks, which do not stop to give them a ride. They run and run.

On roads of white turf and roads of red clay they run. On roads of rocks and roads of mud they run. If they take a wrong step, they do not complain. If they twist their ankles, they do not stop. They are their own doctors. They soothe their twisted ankles with vervain leaves, and their bleeding toes with chewed coffee-tree leaves.

Up and down
Every day
Morning moon
Evening star
Morning star
Evening moon

They run and run, each one on the shadow of another. The morning butterflies brush their powder-covered wings against the children's sweat-dripping faces.

The little palm-tree birds with twigs for their nests follow them from palm tree to palm tree.

The turtledoves and the mourning doves flap their wings to the rhythm of the children's footsteps. And the children run and run.

And up and down
Every day
Morning moon
Evening star
Morning star
Evening moon

Singing their grandparents' last words, humming their uncles' songs, whistling their fathers' tunes, catching the shadows of the birds flying over their heads, seeing their moms' smiling faces, they run and run and run on the Road to A B C.

All are schoolchildren. And to their gentlefolk, they are Toutoun, they are Kousou, they are Loud, they are Preneyis, they are Milsen, they are Dyesèl.

All are schoolchildren.

And up and down every day, morning moon evening star, morning
star evening moon, running left and turning right, counting one and
counting two, learning A and learning B, a hum today, a song tomorrow,

they gaze at the heavens, rise before the sun, sail with the moon,
and dream of stars to read and write and write and read each night and
each morning, each morning and each noon, each noon and each day
one more letter and one more sound, one more sound and one more
word, one more word and one more line, one more line and one more page
of their little songs,

their little songs in the great and beautiful books
on the Road to A B C.